JAPANESE
FAIRY TALES

IWAYA SAZANAMI'S
JAPANESE
FAIRY TALES

THE HOKUSEIDO PRESS

ISBN 0-89346-030-3

Published by The Hokuseido Press
3-12, Kanda-Nishikicho, Chiyoda-ku, Tokyo

PUBLISHER'S NOTE

Iwaya Sazanami is often justly compared to Grimm, for in re-telling old fairy tales of Japan for the children of his country, he did exactly what Grimm did for the German children.

Iwaya no Ojisan or Uncle Iwaya is the name with which the author of the numerous Japanese stories was called by hundreds of thousands of his little readers; his stories have won so much applause from, and have endeared him so much to, the little folks of his country.

The stories contained in this volume were first translated from the Japanese by Miss Ume Tsuda and Mrs. Hannah Riddle and published in 1914. The English edition, however, had long since been out of print, and in 1938 we bought their copyright and republished the stories in twelve beautiful booklets under the editorship of Mr. G. Caiger. The six stories collected here have been selected out of them, the selection being made from the standpoint of popularity for children and for foreign readers.

These stories which have been liked so much by Japanese children will, without doubt, also be liked by children of any country in the world.

CONTENTS

MOMOTARO 9

THE CRAB'S REVENGE 41

THE OLD MAN WHO MADE TREES
   TO BLOSSOM 75

THE TONGUE-CUT SPARROW . . 107

THE TEA-KETTLE OF GOOD LUCK 135

THE STORY OF KACHI-KACHI YAMA 157

MOMOTARO

VERY, very long ago, there lived in a certain place an Old Man and an Old Woman.

One day they both went out in different directions; the Old Man went to the mountain to cut fire-wood and the Old Woman went to the river to do some washing. The Old Woman soon got to the river and set her little washing-tub in a good place,—then she took out of it, one by one, the things she had brought to wash;—shirts stained with perspiration and an old worn-out, unlined gown, and she was washing away when, suddenly, from the upper part of the river, a huge peach, big enough to fill your arms, came plunging and tumbling down the current!

The Old Woman seeing the peach, said, nodding her head as she talked, "Well! well! that is a fine peach! I am sixty years old this year and in all my life I have never yet seen such a large

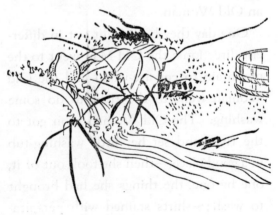

one! I expect it would be very sweet
eating! I will go and pick it up at once
and give it to my Old Man as a present,
—that will be the thing to do," and she
stretched out her hand to the peach but
could not reach it. She looked round
about her in every direction for a stick
but there was not one to be seen. She

did not know what to do. Then she
suddenly thought of a plan!—she turned
towards the peach as it came floating
down the stream, and clapping her hands
in welcome, said:—

> "The distant waters are bitter!
> The near waters are sweet!
> Shun the bitter!
> Come to the sweet!"

This she repeated two or three times.
The peach came on little-by-little,—little-
by-little, and, strange to say, when it got
in front of the Old Woman,—it stopped!!!
She picked it up quickly, hurriedly gathered together her washing, then putting
the peach under her arm she hastened
back to her own house and waited impatiently for her husband's return, thinking, "When my Old Man comes back
how pleased he will be!"

At last, towards evening, the Old Man

came back bearing on his back the firewood which he had cut on the mountain.

Then the Old Woman, running out cried, "My dear Old Man! my dear Old Man! I have been waiting for you to come back for hours!"

"What a fuss you make!" he said. "Has anything happened while I was out?"

"There's nothing the matter," the Old Woman replied, "but I have a lovely present for you which I think you will like when I show it to you."

"Oh indeed," said he, "it's something wonderful no doubt." And then the Old Man having washed his bare feet and legs entered the house.

The Old Woman brought in the peach in both arms, as though it was very heavy, and placed it in front of the Old Man, saying, "Come now! look at this!"

The Old Man on seeing the peach was amazed! "Oh! Oh!" he exclaimed, "this *is* a wonderful peach! Now, without any long story, where did you buy such a peach as this?"

"What do you mean?" cried the Old Woman, "this is not a *bought* peach! it *came* to me and I picked it up!" And then she told the Old Man everything that had happened and he became more and more pleased as he listened. "In that case," he said, "I am more than thankful to have the peach and I think, as I am very hungry, we will make a feast of it at once!"

A big knife was brought from the kitchen and, placing the peach on the chopping-board, they prepared to cut it exactly in half. When, wonderful to tell! from inside the peach there came the voice of a dear little child, saying, "Wait a moment, Mr. Old Man!" and at the same instant the peach split suddenly in half, and a Baby jumped out!

The Old Man and the Old Woman were both so astonished at this appearance, that they were frightened out of their wits, and they fell down,

screaming; but the Baby coming quietly to them said, "Don't be afraid! Don't be afraid! I am not anyone to be nervous about. The truth is, I have been sent down to you by the command of the god of Heaven. Seeing that you are both so sad because you have reached this age without having any children, he also felt sorry for you, and therefore commanded that I should be handed over to you to be brought up as your own child."

The Old Man and the Old Woman were both overjoyed on hearing this.

In that way this child came to be brought up as their own, and as he was born from a peach, the name of "Peach-Boy" was given to him, and all the care which love could give was given to him.

Well! Time passes quickly! and Peach-Boy was soon fifteen years old. One day about then, he went to his Father and kneeling before him very humbly, said, "Father, we became parent and child in a most remarkable manner. Your goodness to me has been higher than the mountain from which you cut grass and deeper than the river in which the washing is done, and there is no way in which I can express my thanks to you."

The Old Man was rather taken aback at this, and said, "Don't speak like that! If we became parent and child, even for a short time, there ought not to be anything very strange in a child receiving kindness from its parents. To offer such thanks in this formal way is too much for me."

Peach-Boy said, "That being the case, I am afraid of saying anything which may seem ungrateful or wilful before returning any of your kindness, but I have a request to make: will you not kindly listen to it?"

The Old Man replied, "You are an exception to other people. Whatever you like to ask I will listen to it." "In that case," said Peach-Boy, "I beg of you to bid farewell to me from now."

"What!" cried the Old Man, "Farewell?"

"Even if we call it 'Farewell'," replied Peach-Boy, "it is but for a short time. I will soon return."

"Then, where do you think of going to?"

"Without knowing everything," said Peach-Boy, "you will not understand, but from earliest times, in a distant part of the sea, there has been an island inhabited by Ogres. Those Ogres do harm in Japan; they take people and eat them! They seize valuable property! And as they are the most hateful creatures in the world, it is my intention to start at once and wage war against them, to catch and crush them and bring back all their treasures.

The Old Man was astonished, for the moment, on hearing these brave words from one so young. But he reflected hopefully, that whatever one might say to the contrary, since this child had been given to him from heaven itself, no accident was likely to happen to him. So he said, with a grunt. "That's capital! if you have such a plan, why should I stop you? And since I will set you free to go according to your wish, hasten across the water to Ogres' Island, and return when you have conquered them."

Peach-Boy was so overjoyed because the Old Man gave his consent so graciously, that he could not wait till the

morrow, but began to prepare to set out on that very day.

The Old Man also set about preparing suitable food for a warrior on a journey. He brought out millet which had been stored away some time before, and placed a big stone mortar on the earthen floor of the kitchen, then with the Old Woman's help, the sound of "pet-ta-ra-ko!" "pet-ta-ra-ko!" soon announced that they had begun to make millet dumplings.

At last the millet dumplings were finished and all Peach-Boy's personal preparations were completed. There was nothing now to hinder his immediate departure as a warrior.

Notwithstanding all this, parting is a sorrowful thing;—and the Old Man and Old Woman, their eyes clouded with tears and with trembling voices, bade him farewell, saying, "Take care of yourself in all your travels, dear one," and, "We shall wait for your joyful return." Peach-Boy too felt the parting deeply, but said only, "Well, I will start now, farewell! take good care of yourselves!" and turned his back on them with his heart full of emotion. Then summoning up all his determination he went quickly out from his home.

Ah! it was bitter! both for the old eyes which followed and for the young eyes which looked back!

Well, Peach-Boy having got over his parting with his parents, went rapidly on his way and just at noontide, being somewhat hungry, he sat down at the foot of a tree by the roadside and brought out one of the millet dumplings prepared for him and began to enjoy it. While thus pleasantly engaged, a spotted dog, as large as a calf, suddenly appeared from a nearby meadow, and came along in a very proud way. He stopped opposite to Peach-Boy and, showing his fangs, growled, and began to threaten him. "You are a daring fellow," he said, "to pass through the territory of the Lord Spotted Dog without even an apology! Leave every bit of the food you have there behind you and go! If you do not I will kill you here on the spot, and bite your head off!" And again he growled threateningly.

Peach-Boy, laughing mockingly, answered, "You wild dog of the woods, what are you talking about! I am travelling for the sake of the country and am on my way to conquer "Ogres' Island." My name is Peach-Boy. If you try to hinder me in any way, there will be no mercy for you; I, myself, will cut you in half from your head downwards!"

At this, the dog, whatever he thought, suddenly put his tail between his legs, and making himself as small as possible, crouched on the ground as though thoroughly frightened, and said, "Then, are you the Lord Peach-Boy of whom I have so often heard? I assure you I had no idea you were he; I beg of you to pardon my rudeness just now!" and, he continued to rub his head on the ground, while he went on. "You say you are passing this way in order to go and conquer Ogres' Island: if you will command me, your humble servant, to accompany you, I shall be grateful for my good fortune."

"Oh! if you wish to go with me," said Peach-Boy, "I will not hinder you."

"Nothing could make me happier than your ready acceptance of my offer," said the dog; "and now, as I am very hungry indeed, won't you please give me one of those things which you were eating just now?"

"These," said Peach-Boy, "are the best millet dumplings in Japan. I cannot give you a whole one, I will give you half-a-one."

"I am grateful to you," replied the dog, and then he accepted the half-dumpling and having eaten it he went on with Peach-Boy. They hurried on as quickly as possible.

They went on and on, through valleys and over mountains. Suddenly from the branches of a tree opposite them, a monkey softly rustling among the leaves, came jumping down, and bowed low before Peach-Boy. He said, "So this is the Lord Peach-Boy! How delightful to see you making a warlike expedition! I pray, let me, your humble servant, accompany you......"

The Spotted Dog, without waiting to hear any more, stared fiercely at the monkey. Growling he said:—"I, Spotted Dog, am accompanying Lord Peach-Boy! Of what use in making war are mountain monkeys like you? Clear out! clear out! I say!" and barking loudly made as though he would bite him.

From the beginning dogs have been on bad terms with monkeys, nor would this monkey on his part, receive such insults quietly. Shewing his teeth and putting out his claws, he was about to fight, when Peach-Boy pushed them both apart, and said, "Wait a moment, you two! Don't be rash! Spotted Dog! restrain yourself a little, sir!"

"Why should I?" objected the dog, "that mountain monkey is defiling your august presence!"

"That is all right! it is nothing to do with you," returned Peach-Boy. First pushing the dog to one side and again turning to the monkey, he said, "Now, who are you?"

The monkey placing his hands on the ground in a respectful position said;—"I am The Monkey of this mountain. As I hear that you, Lord Peach-Boy, are making this journey in order to conquer Ogres' Island, I also wish to be allowed to accompany you."

"You have certainly become a very worthy fellow these days! In that case," continued Peach-Boy, "in consideration of your good intentions, I will give you half of one of the best millet dumplings in Japan, and you may follow me." So saying, he gave to the monkey the half which was left of the dumpling which he had previously given to the dog, and in that way, made the monkey his retainer. Then giving his banner to the dog, he placed him in front, and making the monkey his sword-bearer, he put him behind. Then placing himself between them and carrying in his hand an iron fan, according to the custom of all high military officials in those days, they started peacefully on their way.

By-and-by as they were crossing a moor, all of a sudden, a bird flew out from under their feet. It was a large pheasant, and the dog immediately sprang after it with the intention of making one mouthful of it, but the pheasant thrusting forth its beak prepared to attack the dog.

Peach-Boy seeing this, thought to himself, "Upon my word! this is a most interesting bird! if I can make him my follower he might prove useful!" So he ran to the spot where the contest was going on. Checking the dog, he said in a most threatening manner to the pheasant, purposely speaking in a very loud voice, "What do you mean by getting in the way of my expedition like this? If you surrender, I will take you along with me as my servant; but if you hinder us further, I will set this Spotted Dog on you, and he will twist your head off your neck!"

The bird was very surprised at this and immediately bowed low. With every sign of humility he said, "Can this be Lord Peach-Boy of whom I have so often heard? I am The Pheasant of this moor. I did not know that such a notable Commander-in-Chief was passing this way. I have no words in which to express my apologies for having quarrelled with your honourable retainer, the dog. From this time I follow your commands and offer my formal surrender. Please, I earnestly beseech you to direct my duties as you do those of Mr. Dog and Mr. Monkey." He said this with true humility.

Peach-Boy half-smiling replied, "Such prompt surrender compels my admiration! I now charge you to accompany me in the same way as the dog and the monkey in my expedition to conquer Ogres' Island, and see that you are faithful to me in all things."

"I agree," said the pheasant. Then, as he too had been added to the ranks, and according to precedent, had received half of a millet dumpling, he joyfully went on his way with the others.

The influence of a great General is a wonderful thing! from that time forward, all three animals were the best of friends and obeyed Peach-Boy's commands, heart and soul. And they went on even more rapidly than before.

Always hurrying on and hurrying on, one day they found to their surprise that they had reached the coast. Whichever way they looked there was only the boundless sea to meet their gaze; not even a little island was in sight.

Then Peach-Boy rapidly built a boat, and set out in it with his three retainers for Ogres' Island. Putting up a sail in a fair wind, they slid over the water, and, very soon, Ogres' Island appeared on the horizon.

Looking at the island from the sea, it looked like a rock sharpened with an axe, and on it, was an iron fence with an iron gate. Inside that were several large houses roofed with iron tiles. Truly it seemed a fortress that could never be captured.

Peach-Boy stood in the bow of the boat, and shading his eyes with his hand, was looking at the island. At last calling the pheasant, he said, "As you have wings, fly at once to the island and find out exactly how things are!"

The Pheasant joyfully agreed, and immediately preparing for the journey set off with great spirit. According to his General's commands, he flew as quickly as he could, and at last dropped on to the roof of the castle in the centre of Ogres' Island, when, flapping his wings, he shouted in a loud voice:—"Take heed and listen! all ye ogres who live in this island. The god of Heaven has sent his messenger, General Peach-Boy of Great Japan, to conquer this island! If you desire your lives, at once break off your horns, offer him your treasures and surrender! But if you offer resistance, I, The Pheasant, who now speak, to begin with, and a dog and a monkey, each of them gallant warriors and long practised in the art of using their fangs, will come and bite you to death one by one!"

The ogres on hearing this laughed loudly, and one of them said, "What nonsense! a shallow little moorland pheasant calling out about surrender! Ho! ho! ho—!! it gives me a pain in my side! Come and try the taste of this iron club!" and without staying to arrange his loin-cloth of tiger's skin, he rushed upon the pheasant to strike him down and crush him to powder. Our pheasant was certainly a brave fellow.

He dodged the blow without an effort and with one stroke of his beak on the crown of the ogre's head, stabbed and knocked him down. On seeing this, a red ogre again tried to strike the pheasant with an iron club, but the pheasant in just the same way, with a single stroke of his beak, pierced and broke the ogre's breast-bone. Again, he kicked away with his claws another ogre who was coming at him, and knocking down those who continued to attack him, he fought like fury.

Meanwhile, the dog and the monkey jumping nimbly from the boat and springing to land, at once broke down the large iron front-gates of the garrison and suddenly leaped in, each trying to be first.

Until now the ogres had thought that the enemy consisted of a single pheasant, but when the other two animals came suddenly leaping in, the ogres fought desperately to drive them out. There were red, blue and black little ogres, and they divided into three companies and fought to defend themselves. Their war shouts mingled with the roar of the waves, till it was as though Heaven and Earth were crumbling into fragments.

However, even such ogres as these were becoming gradually weaker, and in the rout that followed, some were drowned in the sea and others, falling on the rocks, were dashed to pieces! The number of those who were struck down and killed by the dog, monkey and pheasant no one can say.

In the end, the only survivor on Ogres' Island was their Chief, the Giant Ogre.

Whereupon, evidently convinced that it was of no use to resist, this Giant

Ogre forthwith threw away his iron-club, broke his own horns, and placed them before Peach-Boy together with his treasures, and prostrating himself like a spider, weakly surrendered. With the tears streaming down in heavy drops, he said humbly," I am filled with admiration at the great power of Lord Peach-Boy! To what purpose shall I offer any further resistance? To-day is the end! I surrender! and only beg of you to spare my life!"

Peach-Boy at once bound this Giant Ogre with cords and made the monkey lead him. To the Dog and the Pheasant he gave the care of the valuable spoil.

In the first place there was a coat, which rendered the wearer invisible! and also a hat possessing the same wonderful power. They began by putting these into a large box, together with a mallet, every blow of which produced pieces of gold! and the sacred coral which the Empress Jingo obtained from the sea; and there were besides,

tortoise-shell and pearls and other precious things.

The Dog and the Pheasant carried this box on their shoulders, and again entering the same boat as before, they joyfully returned victorious from their campaign.

The Old Man and Old Woman had been waiting anxiously for Peach-Boy's return, and their joy needs no description! They with Peach-Boy, had more and more power, and they

lived happily ever after, in the midst
of their ever-increasing dependants and
retainers.

THE
CRAB'S REVENGE

L ONG, long ago, there lived a Monkey and a Crab.

One day these two went out together to enjoy themselves. By-and-by, on the bank of a river, the Monkey picked up the seed of a persimmon, and the Crab found a ball of rice.

The Crab was the first to exclaim— "Oh! see what a nice thing I have found!" Then the Monkey said, "Look what I have picked up too!" He shewed him the persimmon seed, but though he liked persimmons better than anything else, the seed only was not much use. On the other hand, they could eat the ball of rice! For this reason, the Monkey was ready to burst with envy.

Then he considered how he could get hold of the ball of rice. Purposely looking very serious, he said, "I say, Mr. Crab, wouldn't you like to exchange that ball of rice for this persimmon seed?"

The Crab shaking his head said, "I shouldn't like it at all. Your seed is so very tiny. For me to exchange such a big thing as my ball of rice for your seed would be a decided loss to me."

"What you say is very true, Mr. Crab," replied the monkey, "but though the ball of rice is much bigger than the persimmon seed, and also you can eat it at once, yet when you have eaten it, that is the end! there is no further pleasure to be got out of it! You cannot eat this persimmon seed at once I know. But, if you put it into the ground, it will soon become a large tree. Then you will have as many sweet persimmons to eat as you like. Really, I prefer to keep it myself. However, if you don't want to exchange, I won't try to persuade you against your will. I will just take the seed home and plant it myself. But in that case, please remember that by-and-by, when the tree is in fruit, I will not give you *one!*"

With this clever speech he deceived the naturally simple-minded Crab, who replied innocently, "All right, in that case, I will sow it myself and see."

"Very well, then," said the monkey, "we will exchange." Having thus successfully deceived the Crab, he took the ball of rice, and hurriedly eat it up before the Crab could change his mind. After giving the persimmon seed to the Crab as though he was sorry to part with it, they separated for that day.

The Crab returned to his home carrying the persimmon seed with him, and immediately, according to the Monkey's directions, planted it in his garden. In a little while it sprouted, and from two leaves came four; and from five inches it grew to a foot; and as the

days went by it grew bigger and bigger. The Crab was delighted and thought the tree was wonderful; and found his only joy in hoping it would quickly grow large and bear a great deal of fruit.

There is a saying, that peach-trees and chestnut-trees bear fruit in three years, but that persimmon trees need eight years. It was exactly in the eighth autumn from the time that the seed no bigger than the top of your finger was planted, that it had become not only a large tree, but was also covered with most delicious-looking red persimmons, growing in bell-like clusters, just as the Monkey had said it would.

The Crab was beside himself with joy. Wishing to eat some of the persimmons at once, he tried with all his might to reach them from below, of course he was not nearly tall enough and his claws were no use at all. Like all crabs, he used to move sideways, and it seemed very doubtful whether he would ever be able to climb the tree.

At last, in great doubt and perplexity, he folded his claws and thought very hard indeed. He eventually came to the conclusion, that, as he could not do it himself, the best thing to do, was to ask his friend the Monkey to pick the persimmons for him. He went to call on the Monkey at once.

"Are you at home, Mr. Monkey?" he called at the front door. And the monkey's voice answered from inside, "Oh! is that you, Mr. Crab? what a very long time it is since we last met!"

"It is indeed," said the Crab, "and in those eight years the persimmon seed for which I once made an exchange with you has become a very fine tree."

"Now, look at that!" replied the Monkey. "Isn't that just what I said would happen? And it has a lot of fruit too, I expect?"

"Fruit! I should think so indeed! it is simply laden with fruit! And, I say, Mr. Monkey, just listen to me for a moment! I am awfully worried! for although I have such a lot of legs I am no good at climbing trees, and I cannot get at those wonderful persimmons! It will be a great bother for you, but won't you just come over to my place and get them for me? Of course, I will give you some for yourself in return for your trouble."

"Nothing easier!" said the Monkey, "Don't talk of thanks between such good friends! I will come at once and get them for you." And with this they set out together for the Crab's house.

On arriving there, he saw for himself

what he had already heard, that the persimmon had indeed grown into a fine, big tree and was laden with hundreds of red fruit.

"What splendid fruit it has!"—said the Monkey, "and it's a very good kind of persimmon too!"

"Don't waste time talking," exclaimed the Crab, "climb up quickly please, and pick some!"

"All right, I'm not forgetting!" said the Monkey, and he climbed easily up the tree, and immediately picked a persimmon and began to eat it. "Ah!" he cried, "this is excellent! It's as sweet as can be!"

The Crab waiting anxiously below called out, "I say! Isn't it rather bad manners for you to begin eating?"

"What's the matter?" said the Monkey, "I am only trying them for you."

"But you are at it again! Don't eat so greedily all by yourself! Throw some down here too!"

"All right, I'll throw some now!" and the Monkey picked one and threw it. The Crab rushed to pick it up but the first bite gave him a shock, for his teeth were all set on edge by the sourness of the persimmon!

"Oh, this is so sour!" he shouted, "please drop me a really sweet one!"

"Is it? How's this one?"

"Bah! that is just as bad!"

"You grumble at everything!" said the Monkey. "Well then, try this one," and with all his might, he threw down an absolutely green persimmon as hard as a stone. It struck the Crab a terrible blow on the top of his head. Unable to bear the pain, he cried out and fell over, and as he fell there came another blow!

"Aow! Aow! You're hurting me! you're hurting me!" cried the Crab, "what are you doing?"

"You want to know what I am doing? Well, these persimmons all belong to me, every one of them! You had better die without any grumbling! So there!"

There is no doubt, the Monkey was a very violent fellow. He pelted the Crab with green persimmons like a shower of hail, till without any pity he saw the Crab's shell terribly crushed, and the Crab himself at death's door. Then he quickly gathered all the sweet persimmons left on the tree, and carrying them under his arm fled to his own house.

However, the Crab had a son. It so happened that on this day he had gone with some crab-friends to amuse themselves on the edge of a distant swamp. When he came back he was astonished

to find his father lying on the ground
under the persimmon tree in the garden !
His shell and claws had been so badly
hurt that the poor crab was almost dead!

The young crab was overcome with
grief and taking

his father in his claws he called to him loudly, but alas! His father could not speak! In spite of all his loving care the old crab passed away!

There was nothing left to be done but to avenge his father by killing his enemy. But who and where was the villain who had done this murder?

"Surely," he thought, "there must be a clue of some kind!!"

And while looking everywhere, he remembered that until the day before there had been a good number of perfectly ripe persimmons, but that now there was not one left on the tree: there were only sour, green persimmons lying about on the ground.

It looked as though it might have been with those hard green persimmons that his father's shell had been injured.

Presently the young crab slapped his

knee, exclaiming "I have it! The deed was done by that wicked Monkey! there is no doubt about it! My father often used to tell us how, long ago when he was out for a day's pleasure with the Monkey by some river, he exchanged a ball of rice for a persimmon seed which he planted here. Well now, because the Monkey wants to have some persimmons, he has mortally injured my father! He has taken away all the sweet fruit, leaving only the sour ones behind! It is perfectly clear! If he wished to have some persimmons, he had only to ask for them. My father was not the man to refuse to share them!—But to kill him in that brutal way!!—I'll make him sorry for it!" And the young Crab bit his claws in anger.

But when he thought it over again, the enemy certainly was an experienced and terrible animal who had easily killed even his father. How then could he, with his childish strength, pay him out?

This thought made the brave young crab so sad that for a time he could not think what to do. Suddenly he remembered his father's old and good friend, the Mortar. Now this Mortar was formerly a partner in the stone wall in which his father had lived. Later on he had been discovered by a human being and had been turned into a Mortar. He was by nature very faithful, and as he never failed to carry out anything he undertook for others, the young crab thought that if his help were asked he would probably give it. And he hurried off at once to the Mortar's house.

He saw the Mortar and with tears told him of the way the Monkey had treated his father. The Mortar was very sorry indeed.

"This is indeed a shocking affair!" he said. "You must feel it terribly, but don't be in the least bit anxious about your father

being avenged. I will attend to that!"
And he comforted him in every way he
could. But thinking that after all, the
enemy was the Monkey whom he could
not attack lightly, the Mortar sent a
messenger to his old friends, the Roast-
chestnut and the Hornet to ask them
both to come and see him. The former
was a Musketry Instructor and the latter
a Master of the Lance.

When the Roast-chestnut and the
Hornet, in answer to the Mortar's mes-
sage, came to see what he wanted, he
said to them, "I must apologise for
troubling you to come here to-day, but
there is something about which I wish
to consult you. It is in connection with
Mr. Crab (the father of this young
gentleman whom you see here) who was
a very dear friend of mine. To put it
shortly, the Monkey for his own reasons,

has murdered him! I should like to find some way in which to help this young Mr. Crab to avenge him. And therefore, my friends, I asked you to come here, as I want to beg your help in this matter. Will you not lend me a hand to kill this wicked Monkey?"

The Roast-chestnut on hearing this drew nearer, and said, "From what you have said I believe that the cause of the quarrel was the fruit of the persimmon, one of our genus. In that case, it is a right and proper thing that I, one of the fruit-family, should support Mr. Crab, as an apology is due to him from our clan. If there is anything I can possibly do, please command me!"

The Hornet on hearing this offer felt that he could do no less, and said, "I have always thought that Monkey was a rude fellow. He has destroyed my

house many times. And if what you
say is true, I will join you, and I will
certainly pierce him with the spear of
my hatred!" And as they all thus
cheerfully assumed responsibility, the
Mortar was very delighted.

"I have a plan in my head," said he,
"but I wonder how it would answer!"

"Do tell us what it is!"
cried the Roast-chestnut
and the Hornet, both
speaking together.

"Then come
nearer," said the

Mortar, "come nearer!" And as "in
the multitude of counsellors there is
wisdom," these three put their heads
together and entered earnestly into con-
sultation.

While talking quietly there, it seems
they settled all their
arrangements,

for presently the Mortar said, "Now whatever happens, don't let there be any mistakes!"

"Trust us for that!" replied the other two; and they separated for that day in the gayest of spirits. But the Mortar, who had been a very great friend of the dead Crab's, returned with his son to the house and assisted him in everything concerned with his father's funeral.

The Monkey, though he had been so brutal to the Crab and stolen all the sweet persimmons, and was very pleased with himself, nevertheless knew quite well that he had been very wicked, and thought it probable that everybody connected with the Crab's household bore him ill-will.

Moreover, when he thought that perhaps they would come out to get their revenge, he felt rather frightened. For the time being, he stayed at home, hiding in his house, wearily watching the days go by.

However, being the impudent fellow he was, he began to think something like this. " Perhaps, after all, this worry is not necessary. When I threw persimmons at the Crab, there was not a single creature near, so no one else can possibly know that I did it——! And if no one knows, there is no need at all for me to be anxious or afraid."

Thus arguing to keep his courage up, one day he went cautiously into the neighbourhood of the Crab's dwelling, and while pretending to pay no particular attention to his surroundings, he tried to find out how the land lay. Everything seemed to be just as he had imagined. The crabs certainly did not bear any ill-will towards the Monkey. They supposed that the father Crab, wishing to get some persimmons himself, had climbed the tree in spite of great difficulties, but that the weight of his shell had made him slip, and that he had fallen down head foremost, when the half-ripe persimmons falling in a shower, had struck and killed him. His household were all resigned to the fact and bore no grudge against anybody.

The Monkey was greatly relieved, and indulged in all manner of pleasant reflections, thinking too, that it would have been as well if he had gone to express his sympathy at the time and pretended to know nothing about how it had happened.

However, one day a messenger came to him from the Crab. Before asking him his business he showed him to the guest-room. In answer to his questions, the messenger very politely replied:

" A few days ago the Father Crab had thought he would like some persimmons. If he had waited for the others it would have been all right, but he climbed the tree himself. Not being used to it, sad to say, he had suddenly lost his footing and fallen down head first, and so had been killed outright. Therefore his young master had directed him to say that, as the persimmon tree in their garden was of no use to them, they hoped the Monkey would accept it as a legacy. He had come to invite him to go and see it."

The Monkey on hearing this pretended to be greatly surprised and said, " What is that ? Do you mean to say that Mr. Crab has fallen from the persimmon tree in his garden, and is dead ! Dear me ! Dear me ! I can hardly believe it ! ! This is the first I have heard of it ! It is indeed a shocking affair! To tell the truth, Mr. Crab and I have been friends from childhood, and it is just eight years ago that he and I went out for a day's pleasure together by the riverside and we made an exchange of a ball of rice which he had picked up and of a persimmon seed which I had. Probably the persimmon tree which you speak of has grown from that very seed! As you see, I am personally concerned in this matter, and I am more than sorry for you all!!"

And then the Monkey cried loudly pretending to be very sorry. The false tears ran down his cheeks in large drops!

The Crab's messenger, seeing this, thought to himself, "Whereabouts did he pinch himself to produce such sounds? Wait a little! he will shed real tears before long!!" but he did not show his feelings, he kept his polite attitude and said, "Your grief is very natural, and it will, I am sure, rejoice Father Crab in his grave. But will you not agree to the request which has now been put before you?"

"Of course I will agree," said the Monkey. "Not knowing anything of what had happened, I have not yet been to offer my sympathy, and as I wish to apologize for that, I will take this opportunity and go at once."

Then, having said goodbye to the messenger, he made his own preparations and immediately set out for the Crabs' house.

When he got there he saw that all the Crabs and their friends had come out to meet him, and with the most careful regard to etiquette were ranged to the right and left of the stone wall, bowing low before him.

The Monkey's sense of importance rose at once! Speaking as though he were addressing his inferiors, he said, " You should not have troubled! Much obliged! Much obliged!" Then in a proud way he strutted to the hall-door.

Here again a servant appeared and directly he saw the Monkey invited him to come in, and bowing slightly, led the way from the corridor to the guest-room and showed him to the seat which had been prepared in his honour.

The Monkey having taken the seat to which he was led, rested for a short time, and then Mr. Young-Crab, the master of the house, appeared and saluted him with due politeness.

"I presume you are Mr. Young-Crab," said the Monkey. "This recent sad event is indeed a very terrible affair. You have my sympathy!" And putting on airs he continued to sympathize.

In the meantime preparations having been made to offer him food and wine, the Monkey was uncommonly pleased and heedlessly yielding to the urgent invitations of his host he gorged himself without realising it.

Then he was conducted to the tea-room at the back of the house that he might be served with tea from the water boiled there, and Young-Crab, politely begging him to make himself at home and rest at his ease for a short time, bowed and withdrew. He waited for what seemed a very long time but his host did not return.

"I have always heard," he thought,

"that the tea ceremony was a tedious affair, ... it's an awful nuisance to be kept waiting like this! If they don't give me something to drink very soon, my throat will be dried up!"

His throat was really burning, as he recovered from the effects of his intoxication, and unable to endure it any longer, he thought he would help himself to at least a cup of hot water, although it was bad manners! He went to the fire-place and just as he put his hand to the lid of the kettle which hung over it, the previously mentioned Roast-chestnut, who had been patiently biding his time in the hot ashes, burst forth with a loud report and hit the Monkey in the neck!

Taken by surprise, with a scream the Monkey fell down; but being naturally a stubborn sort of fellow, he was not likely to be much affected by a single shot.

Pressing the place and screaming "Oh it burns! it burns!" the Monkey rushed from the tea-room, when the Hornet, who had been lying in wait in the eaves, working a large-headed spear through his hand with a hissing sound, suddenly thrust it at the Monkey's cheek and stabbed him!

Because of these attacks the Monkey was at his wits' end, and holding his head in his hands fled as fast as he could to the front of the house. Here our old friend, the Mortar, was hiding on the top of the wall, and as the Monkey came running out, he jumped upon his head and pinned him down so tightly that even such a monkey could not move! He could only lie there groaning in his pain.

Then the master, Young-Crab, appeared in front of the Monkey, flourishing the shears which he had inherited from his father, and mocked at his condition, saying, "Well, mountain monkey! what do you think of it now?"

The Monkey gasped out, "Do you still .... think that I am .... the .... murderer .... of your .... father?"

"That does not need putting into words," said Young-Crab. "You were so cruel and brutal to my father that he died!"

"No," said the Monkey, "he only met with his deserts! . . . . ."

"Do you still dare to say such a thing? You shall not say that again!!" And opening wide his shears, Young-Crab snipped off the Monkey's head and so successfully accomplished his *revenge!*

THE OLD MAN
Who Made Trees to Blossom

ONCE upon a time, just when or where is not known, there lived an old couple. They were happy but for one thing, and that was they had no children. And so, not to be entirely alone, they kept a dog whose name was Shiro, and to Shiro they gave almost a parent's love.

We hear that a cat forgets the kindness of three years in three days, while dog remembers a kindness of three days for three years.   There are few animals, at all events, which remember a good turn as long as a dog.   Since the old man and the old woman loved Shiro as their own child, he in his turn was grateful for their love and was entirely devoted to them.   In the day time Shiro trotted after his master as he went to the mountains to cut fire-wood.   At night he faithfully guarded his house and fields.   So day by day the old people grew more fond of Shiro.   If ever they had any thing extraordinarily good to eat, they would first give him a treat, even if they had none for themselves, for nothing rejoiced them so much as the sight of Shiro's happy face.

Next door there lived another old couple, but they, I am sorry to say, were of quite another sort, and they hated Shiro.   If he so much as peeped in at

their kitchen door, it was enough to
make them shout at him angrily as if,
indeed, they had already been robbed of
their fish; or they would throw pieces
of wood or anything else that
happened to be at hand.
Many was the time
that poor Shiro
ran limping
home.

One day, for some strange reason, Shiro kept up a continual barking in the field behind the house, so the old man, thinking that perhaps his old enemies the crows were making some mischief, went out to see. At first Shiro jumped excitedly on his master, then taking the old man's *kimono** in his teeth, he pulled him to a corner of the field, where he began to scratch the ground with great vigour under a large elm tree. The old man was greatly puzzled at Shiro's actions. "Why Shiro," he said, "what is the matter with you?"

Shiro, still smelling the ground, began to bark, "Bow-wow! Dig here! Bow-wow! Dig here!"

Then at last the old man understood that Shiro wanted him to dig, because there was really something hidden under

* Dress.

the elm tree. So he said, "Oh, very well, I understand." At once he fetched a spade from the barn and as soon as he had thrust it deep into the earth, in the place where Shiro had begun to dig, the spade touched something which gave a clanging sound, and at the same time he saw something bright and glittering.

"What can this be?" exclaimed the old man, as he reached down and took something out of the ground. Who will believe me? It was a gold coin.

Thinking all this most wonderful, the old man kept on digging, and the longer he dug, the more coins kept streaming out, till soon there was quite a mountain of them. The old man was thunder-struck. He went quickly for his wife, and together they managed to carry home all the coins.

Of course the good old people kept

them all,—and why not,—for they came from their own field. Thus in a day, thanks to this good luck, they had become very rich.

The next day the troublesome old neighbour came and very politely asked if he might borrow Shiro for a little while.

The old man thought it strange that his neighbour should come to borrow Shiro, when he had always treated him so cruelly before, but he was good-natured and obliging, so he said, "Certainly, if he can be of any use to you, take him and welcome." So Shiro was lent to the neighbour.

That wicked old man, pleased with his success, came home with a self-satisfied smile on his face, and said to his wife, "See, old lady, I persuaded the old man to lend me his dog, and now, only think of the riches he will bring us. Get me my spade at once." The next moment spade in hand, he was hurrying out into the field behind the house, where there

stood just such an elm tree as his neighbour's. Then he said to the newly-bor-
rowed Shiro, "Look here, Shiro, if there
are gold coins in the ground under your
own elm tree, why should there not be
some under mine? Now, dig here and
see—or here, or here," roughly taking
Shiro by the neck he rubbed his nose
into the ground as he spoke, so that the
poor dog was forced to dig whether he
would or not. So Shiro in great pain
began to scratch the ground with his
fore paws. Then the old neighbour
was delighted and exclaimed,—"Oh, it's
here, is it? here? Well, then I need
you no longer. Get away. I will dig for
myself now." Then he spat on his
palms and with might and main drove
the spade into the earth. "Why, how
is this?" he soon cried rather anxiously,
"no gold coins in sight yet? Well, I'll

work a little longer." But though he
turned over two or three spadefuls of
earth, nothing, not even a pair of *zori**
came to light—to say nothing of gold
coins.

"They must be well hidden," he grumbled, still working away. Just then all
at once horrid black mud gushed out
and filled the hole which he had been
digging.

Seeing the mud the old
man was furious with
rage and then he
turned on Shiro;
"Confound you,
wretch," he
screamed,
"you are
the worst
rascal !

---

* Straw sandals.

The idea of treating your neighbours to mud, when you manage to get gold coins for your master. You shall pay dearly for this." With that he struck Shiro an ugly blow with the spade, which the

poor dog was unable to dodge. It was Shiro's death-blow. He staggered and fell dead. The old man threw the body into the hole and covered it well over with earth. Then he went back to the house, looking as if nothing unusual had happened.

As time went by and Shiro did not come home, the old people began to feel anxious, and thinking there could be no harm in going to fetch him, the old man went to his neighbour's house. " What is our dog, Shiro, doing?" he inquired. " Please return him to me if you have done with him," he added earnestly.

But the neighbour sat there quite brazen-faced and said, " Oh, it is Shiro you are after, is it? Well, I killed him the other day."

" What, killed Shiro!" The old man was aghast. " Why, why did you kill him?"

Then the neighbour began insolently to reply. "I am not the kind of man who would kill an innocent creature. Listen to me. I borrowed him the other day and charged him to guard my field, for I have had a good deal of trouble of late from those wretched foxes, but he was so disobedient that he neglected his task and did nothing but eat and sleep all day. And besides he injured my property. I was naturally provoked, and I confess that I was a little rough with him. Although he was very dear to you, could you yourself have stood calmly by while he was making such trouble for other people?"

When the old man heard these words he began to cry bitterly, "Oh, my poor little dog!" he sobbed. "If I had known of all this at the time, I would have come

and made the humblest apologies
if I might only have saved Shiro's life!
Oh, how cruel!" For a time he gave

way to his grief, but at last resigning
himself to his loss he said;
"Of what use is it to cry
over what is done for?
If Shiro did wrong of
course he deserved to
die, and we cannot
help it now. But at
least I should like
to take his body
home with me.
You will surely

give it to me."

"That is not possible," the neighbour returned, "for it is now several days since I buried him underneath the elm tree in my field."

"What shall I do then?" said the poor old man, "for of course I do not wish to dig the body up after it has once been buried." He was silent for a while, then suddenly a thought came to him and he asked, "Would it be too much to ask you to sell me the elm tree?"

"My elm tree?" asked the neighbour in some surprise. "Certainly, if you want it, there is no reason why I should not sell it. But what do you want with it?"

"It is natural," the old man replied, "that I should think fondly of it, since Shiro is buried under it. Please sell it to me, I beg of you."

"If you want it so very much, take it by all means," said the neighbour.

So the old man bought the elm tree and thanking his neighbour he took it home weeping, knowing that he was carrying Shiro's body.

Now what do you think he did with the tree? He made a large mortar and pestle out of it, and soon he began to pound *awa-mochi*.*

The old man pounded and the old woman helped him by mixing the *mochi* in the mortar. "Dear Shiro," they said, "we will make you the *awa-mochi* you are so fond of. Be patient and wait." They talked in this way to Shiro just as if were with them.

Now a very strange thing happened. The first *sho*† of millet which was put into the mortar immediately swelled to

---

* Millet cakes.   † 1½ quarts.

two *sho*, then three *sho*, and more and more, so that without putting any more millet into the mortar a perfect stream of *awa-mochi* came pouring out.

The old people were astonished and delighted at the sight of this, and thinking it might be the work of their dead Shiro, trying to show his gratitude to them they both tasted some of it. They had never tasted anything half so delicious, and then it was so satisfying that after eating one piece, they had no desire to eat for a day afterwards.

How the old neighbour got wind of this, no one knows, but at any rate it was not long before he came poking his nose in at the door saying, "I am very sorry to trouble you, but would you lend me your mortar and pestle for a little while, for I also am anxious to pound *awa-mochi*?" So you may see what the artful old neighbour was about.

The poor old man, knowing by sad experience his neighbor's free and easy way of borrowing other people's property, was not very cordial to him. But then he reflected that the mortar and pestle had been made from the elm tree which he had bought of him and he felt he could not decently refuse his request. So reluctantly he let his treasure go. This time again days passed and there was no sign of any one coming to return the borrowed mortar.

The old man fearing lest something had happened, became quite uneasy, so at last he went to his neighbor's house and asked him very politely if he had done with the mortar. The old neighbour was sitting in front of his oven, busily burning something. He looked up as he heard the old man's voice and said quite calmly, "Oh, that mortar is it? Why, I have broken that to pieces and now I am burning it."

"What! you are burning my mortar!" exclaimed the old man quite horrified.

"Of course, you understand," answered the other, "I should not have burned it without good reason, especially as it was borrowed, but as I was pounding the other day, horrid black mud came out of it and spoiled my nice *awa-mochi*, which I had made with such pains. That is why I broke it, and you see me burning it here!"

"Black mud!" exclaimed the old man astonished.

"Yes, black mud. At every stroke of the pestle it streamed out of the mortar."

"I am very sorry" said the old man, "but if you had only told me about it, I would gladly have given you some of my own *awa-mochi*. How could you have been so quick-tempered! But talking is of no use now that the mortar is destroyed. But I will ask you to give me some of the ashes."

"If ashes are all you want, take as much as you like."

The old man filled a basket and went home, but as he was of an amiable disposition he bore his neighbour no grudge. He immediately took the ashes and without knowing quite what he was doing he began sprinkling them all over the garden.

Suddenly a marvellous thing happened. All the bare, naked plum-trees and cherry-trees burst into full bloom, although it was not yet spring time. It was a beautiful sight. The old man was amazed and began clapping his hands and exclaiming with delight. The ashes

which were left in the basket he put carefully away.

One day a strange knight came to
the gate and called loudly for admit-
tance. The old man went out himself to

see who was there.

The stranger accosted him with these words: "I am a retainer of the prince of this province. His highness' favourite cherry-tree died not long ago. No amount of care and nourishment could keep it alive. His highness in consequence is quite upset and takes no interest in life, and we, his attendants, are very anxious about him. By good luck we heard the other day of some wonderful ashes in your possession which can make even dead trees blossom. If you really have these ashes, I beg you to come with me to the castle, and see if you cannot do something for this tree." The knight was very pressing.

The old man was bewildered at first by the knight's sudden appearance and his unusual request, but he answered: "Yes, all you say is true. I have those wonderful ashes and why should I refuse his highness' request? I will gladly go with you and I think the prince will soon see his favourite cherry-tree in full bloom."

The knight was grateful for the old man's prompt response, and begged him to hasten with him to the castle. So they set out at once, the knight walking ahead, and the old man following with the basket of ashes. In good time they reached the castle.

There they found the prince waiting impatiently and no sooner did he see the old man's face than he began!— "Welcome, my good fellow. Forgive my impatience, but will you not set to work at once on my poor cherry-tree? I will watch you from here."

"With your permission I will begin now," replied the old man. Then after a few simple preparations, he quietly took the basket of ashes, climbed up into the cherry-tree and seated himself in a convenient place. Taking a handful of ashes, he threw them up over the top of the tree. Then strange as it may seem, the branches which till then had been as dead as fire-wood, suddenly began to blossom and the beauty of the flowers almost blinded their eyes! You can fancy how pleased the prince was. He jumped for joy, and remembering that this was all due to the old man's kindness, he summoned him and rewarded him with gold and silver, of course, but beside that he gave him quite a mountain of beautiful raiment and furniture and other treasures. But most important of all he gave him a new name for luck saying, "You deserve to be called Old Man Flower-Blower hereafter."

Soon after this the old man took leave

of the prince and went home in high spirits.

Soon it came to the ears of the disagreeable neighbour that the old man had received from the prince the title of Old Man Flower-Blower and many rare gifts beside, in return for his valuable services in bringing the cherry-tree to life. He was filled with envy at his good fortune, and after prying about in his usual inquisitive fashion, he found out that the cause for it all was nothing more than the ashes from the mortar which he had burned! "Well!" he exclaimed. "Those ashes! Who would have thought it? Why should I not try my hand at that business as well as my neighbour? And this time I have no need to borrow from him, for there are surely some of those ashes still about." Quickly he raked his oven and gathered a basketful, just as if they were some rare treasure. It would have been better for him if he had left them where they were, as you shall see. With his basket on his arm he ran out into the street crying; "Ei! I am the famous Old Man Flower-Blower, I will make your old dead trees blossom!" causing quite a commotion wherever he went.

Now it happened that the prince heard the old neighbour's cry and he said to his retainers, "It seems to me that I hear our old friend, Old Man Flower-Blower passing by. Let us call him in to relieve the monotony of a weary day, and he shall amuse us, by making our trees blossom."

The attendants went out at once to fetch the old man in.

He was, of course, in high glee thinking that now all his wishes were about to come true.

At sight of him the prince suspected that something was wrong. "Was it you," he asked, "who, but now, passed our gate crying, 'Old Man Flower-Blower'?" "It was I, your highness," the old man replied with overwhelming politeness.

"That is strange," said the prince, quite puzzled. "I know of only one Old Man Flower-Blower, but I dare say you may be a disciple of his."

"Oh no," quickly rejoined that deceiver, "I am the real Old Man Flower-Blower, and the one who came to your castle was my disciple."

"This is most interesting," said the prince. "If you are the principle Old Man Flower-Blower, then your skill must be something quite over-powering. Luckily there stands a dead tree yonder. Make it blossom."

Now the old man thought his chance had come at last, and he hurried to the tree. Taking a handful of ashes, he sprinkled them over it exclaiming *yatto, yatto,* but the tree remained just as before. To say nothing of blossoms, not even a bud appeared! Then the old man

began pouring on more ashes, thinking that perhaps the first had not been enough.

But all in vain. Again and again he

tried, throwing the ashes with might and main. But not a blossom came. And the ashes were scattered all over the garden and at last they flew into the eyes and nose of the prince till he could bear it no longer. Quite beside himself with rage he cried out—"Out with you, false Flower-Blower! How dared you deceive me, you rascal? Arrest him, my men!"

It was not long before the wretch was safe in prison.

But Shiro's master became richer every day, thanks to the gold which he had dug from under the elm tree, and to the bounty of the prince. He lived in peace and happiness, known far and wide as the famous Old Man Flower-Blower. *Medetashi!*

THE
TONGUE-CUT SPARROW

ONCE upon a time there lived an old man and his wife. The old man was of a kindly nature and had a pet sparrow which, since he was child-less, he treated as tenderly as if it had been his own child.

One day the old man took a basket and a hatchet in his hand and went as usual to the mountains to cut fire-wood. The old woman in the meantime began to wash clothes at the well.

After she had washed for some time
she found she wanted some starch, so
she went into the kitchen to fetch it.
But what do you think had happened?
All the starch she had made
that morning was

gone and the dish was empty.

"Dear me!" she said, "I wonder who can have stolen the starch I made so carefully. Some horrid fellow, I suppose! And yet how? No one has been here for hours." Saying this and feeling much puzzled she began to look about her, until the sparrow in the cage in the corner of the room, called out:

"What are you looking for, my old mistress?"

"Nothing," she answered, "only I cannot help wondering why the starch is all gone when I saw it here only a few moments ago." "O!" said the sparrow, "I helped myself to that starch." "What!" she cried, "did you eat the starch?"

"Yes, mistress, to tell the truth, I did," he replied. "You see I did not know it was such useful stuff, nor did I know that it was wrong to eat it, since it was in the dish out of which I sometimes feed. It was very careless of me, but please forgive me."

Yet, though the Sparrow frankly confessed his fault and begged her pardon over again and again, the old woman only grew more and more angry. She had never loved the bird and had always treated him harshly.

"You hateful thing!" she cried. "How could you eat up my carefully prepared starch? See how I shall punish you!" Saying this she took a pair of scissors and though the bird with tears in his eyes was still praying for mercy, she took him out of his cage and cut his tongue out! "Was this the tongue that licked my starch?" she cried. "Now I am fully avenged! Get out of my house!"

Meanwhile the old man little dreaming of what had happened at home, went on cutting wood on the mountain. At last he said to himself, "Today's work is done; so now I will go home to see my dear little sparrow again."

Toward evening he reached home, looking forward eagerly to seeing the bird. But when he looked into the cage he could not see his little sparrow, for the cage was empty. The old man thought this strange. He asked his wife where the bird was, but she pretended to be silly and to know nothing about it. "I don't know where he is," said she. "But don't you see," said the old man, "that he is not in the cage?"

"Is that so?" she answered. "Well then, I suppose he must have flown away somewhere." And saying this she tried to look as if it was nothing to do with her.

"Nonsense!" cried the old man, who

was getting more and more excited. "Why would so tame a bird fly away by himself? You must have done something to make him fly off when I was away. Now tell me exactly what you did to him."

When the point was reached in this way the old woman could do nothing but tell the truth; so she said, "While you were away, my husband, the bird ate up my carefully prepared starch, so I cut out his tongue and drove him away."

When the old man heard this, his grief knew no bounds. "Oh, poor little thing!" he cried. "He was only a bird and meant no harm in eating your starch. When you could have forgiven him so easily, how could you have been so cruel as to cut out his tongue and drive him away? If I had been here he should never have been punished so severely;

this cruel deed was done because I was away. Alas! alas!" The old man cried as bitterly as if he had lost a child.

So early the next morning he went forth to seek his lost pet, entirely neglecting his work and paying no heed to his wife's advice not to go.

And as he went along seeking his favourite, he sang:

"Tongue-cut sparrow
        where are you?
Where is your lodging?
        where are you?
Tongue-cut sparrow,
        chu, chu, chu."

The Sparrow soon recognized the voice of the master who had cared for him for so many years, and came out of his house to meet him.

"Is it you, my dear old master?" he cried, "it is kind of you to come to look for me."

"Ah! here you are at last!" cried the old man joyfully. "I could not restrain my longing for you, so I came to seek you."

"How can I ever thank you enough?" said the Sparrow affectionately. "But why stand in the road? Please enter my humble cottage." Saying this he led the old man into his house.

The house was made of bamboo bush as sparrow's houses always are, and though the pillars and roof were of bamboo too, the cottage seemed neat and roomy. The sparrow led the old man along and asked him to enter the parlour and thanked him again politely for his kindness in calling on him. "I think," the sparrow said, "I deserve your anger for having eaten my mistress's starch without asking her leave; yet you do not blame me at all, but come a long way to see me. I do not know how to thank you enough; these tears you see are tears of joy!"

"No, no," said the old man waving his hand from right to left, "another old man might have scolded you, but I, on the contrary, loving you more than a child of my own, reproached my wife for the wrong she did in driving you away, with your tongue cut out for a fault so small as that of eating starch. I have never felt more delighted than in finding you happy here." And his face betrayed his heartfelt joy.

The sparrow was anxious to give as much pleasure as possible to the kind and generous master who had come from so far to see him, so he entertained him with a feast which was prepared by his family with the greatest care. To add to the jollity the sparrows danced the "Sparrow Dance," a favourite dance of theirs.

This pleased the old man very much, and he said that he had never enjoyed himself so much before in all his long life. So happy was he that he felt as if he were in paradise.

While he was enjoying himself in this way, it was gradually getting darker. When the old man noticed this he said, "You have given me such pleasure that I feel ten years younger. But now, I must say goodbye, for the sun has nearly set."

But the sparrow would not let him go

and said, "Why are you in such a hurry? If it grows too dark for you to go home, can't you stay overnight? We should feel very happy if you would stay several days in this humble hut of ours. Until now I have always received your most tender care and I do not think I can ever repay one thousandth part of it by entertaining you for a day or two. Won't you please stay?"

"No," answered the old man, "thank you so much for your kindness, but I have to return to-day, as I must not be away from home too long. I shall often visit you in the future and I hope you will show me as interesting a dance as I saw to-day."

"Then you really must go?" said the sparrow. "How I wish I could keep you! but if you must go, please wait a minute." And bringing forward two rattan baskets, the sparrow continued. "I really don't want you to go, dear old master, for after your long journey, I have not entertained you in such a way as to prove my gratitude fully. Now here are two rattan baskets; one heavy, the other light. Take whichever one you like home with you as a present."

"A present?" said the old man. "No. I could not be so mean as to take a present home after having had such a wonderful time. Nevertheless, your offer ought not to be slighted, so I will take one of the baskets with me."

"Will you take the heavier one?" asked the sparrow.

"No, no," answered the old man, "I am old and cannot carry a heavy load; the lighter one will do well enough."

"Then please take the lighter one," said the sparrow.

So the old man putting the lighter basket on his shoulder with the sparrow's help, went and stood at the gate, together with the birds who had come to see him off.

"Good-bye, sparrow dear, I will be back again before long," said the old man.

"I expect you to come back again soon," said the sparrow. Good-bye! Take care of yourself on the road."

So the old man started off, often looking back as he went along, while the sparrow watched him grow smaller and smaller till he was out of sight, for they had parted from each other sorely against their will.

But now let us turn and look at the old woman. She had been left at home alone all day and was growing tired of waiting for her husband. "I suppose my old man must be looking for that mischievous sparrow," she grumbled, "I cannot understand why he does it." Saying this she went and stood at the gate waiting for her husband to return.

By and by the old man came home carrying the rattan basket on his back.

"How can you be so late?" asked the cross old woman angrily.

"Oh, don't scold me," said her husband wiping away the sweat and putting down his burden. "I had a wonderful time at the sparrow's house and have brought back a present as well. The sparrow gave me two baskets from which to choose; one heavy, the other light; and I chose the lighter one rather than

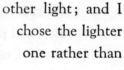

the heavier, which I thought would be too heavy for me to carry. Open it and see what is inside," he added.

"In truth," said the old woman suddenly becoming cheerful, "you enjoyed yourself then. Let us see what is inside," she continued. Without so much as troubling herself to give the tired old man a cup of tea, she hastened to take off the cover and open the basket. What do you think they saw there? Beautiful garments and costly treasures, to say nothing of gold, silver and precious stones!

When the old man saw these things he began to dance with joy, the sparrow-dance he had seen that day; but the old woman frowned and said: "How dull-witted you are! Why did you not bring back the heavier basket? You have no sense!"

"How can you say so?" said the old

man. "Are not these enough? You are too grasping, my old woman."

"But what a fool you were to take the lighter one when you might have had the heavier one. Well, I will go now and fetch that heavy bundle." So saying she got up to go.

"Stop! stop!" cried the old man, "it will do no good," and he tried to prevent her from going. But the old woman did not listen to his words and tucking up the skirts of her garments, she took the old man's staff and she set forth. As she hurried along she repeated the same song as the old man:

"Tongue-cut-sparrow,
where are you?
Where is your lodging?
Chu, chu, chu."

Meanwhile, after the old man had gone, the door of the sparrow's house had been locked and the family were now talking among themselves about the old man and woman, "He is truly a good old man," said the Tongue-cut Sparrow. "How shall we entertain him next time he comes, I wonder? How different his ill-natured wife is from him! She is as cruel as can be, for she drove me away with my tongue cut for so small a fault as licking starch."

At that moment there was a knock at the door and a voice called out sneezing, (for they say people sneeze when they are backbitten by others), "Is this the house of the Tongue-cut Sparrow?" When the sparrow went to see who it was, he found the old woman who had cut his tongue, standing at the door, for as the proverb says: "Speak of an angel and you hear the rustle of his wings."

When the sparrow saw her, though

very angry at having had his tongue cut out, yet felt he ought to be grateful to her as she had been his mistress for so long a time; "Welcome, dear mistress, please come in," he cried, and was about to lead her in when the old woman stopped him saying, "Please don't trouble, for I am in a hurry and must go at once."

"But won't you come in and rest a little while?" said the sparrow, "you have come so far."

"No, thank you," said the old woman, "I have to go home at once, so don't trouble yourself about a dinner or a sparrow dance, but instead I will take a present home with me." "Very well," said the sparrow, "I will give you a present, but I am sorry there is only a heavy basket left as your husband took the light one home."

' Never mind," said the old woman, "I am much younger and stronger than my old man and would rather have the heavier bundle; so please bring it to me at once."

"Very well, I will bring it," said the sparrow and soon he carried a large rattan basket, which seemed very heavy, from an inner room.

The old woman took the present and put it on her back with many an 'Ah!' and 'Oh!' and then went out without thanking him properly only saying, "That's all. Good-bye."

Now this rattan basket was twice as

heavy as the large stone which was used as a weight to press radish pickle in her home. Even such a woman as this was filled with wonder at the weight. Sweat came rolling down her face in big drops and as she walked she groaned with pain.

There was, however, in her heart a strong hope that she would find great treasure in this heavy basket; and this made her walk with all her energy. But in spite of this her burden was getting too heavy to carry, and her desire to see the contents of the basket too strong to resist, so she could not wait until she reached home but determined to open it on the way.

So she put the basket down by the roadside and took off the cover. What do you think she found there? No treasure, but a monster with three eyes, a giant toad, a viper, some larvae, a mantis, and other terrible reptiles and slimy creatures which wriggled round in the basket.

The old woman was terrified. Her knees were like water. She fell to the ground with a shriek.

When these dreadful creatures heard the scream they slowly lifted up their heads. First of all the viper crawled out of the basket and wound itself about her hands and feet. Then the toad began to lick her cheeks.

The old woman was desperate, she screamed and screamed for help. At last she escaped from them. She fell down many times and stumbled over things all the way home. It was all she could do to get there at all.

When she told the old man what had happened, he was not surprised, but said, "Did not I tell you not to be too greedy? You have been justly punished."

And by degrees he brought her to see her own sin and to be really sorry for it. The story goes on to say that after that time she was as good as the good old man, for which, God be thanked.

THE TEA-KETTLE OF
GOOD-LUCK

ONCE upon a time there was a
temple called Morinji in Tate-
bayashi in the province of Kodzuke.
The abbot of this temple was very fond
of ceremonial tea, so that he took delight
in making it every day.

One day he bought a new tea-kettle.
It was so extraordinarily beautiful and so
well shaped, that he was highly pleased
with his bargain and felt sure that this

was quite the best kettle in the world.

One day he took it out of its usual place and began examining it, turning it round and round.

"Certainly this is a fine tea-kettle," he said, "I must invite some guests shortly to ceremonial tea, and astonish them all with it."

While he was musing in this way, he began to feel strangely drowsy, and gradually his head dropped on to his desk and he fell into a doze.

Then a most extraordinary thing happened. The tea-kettle which he had set upon its box, began stealthily to move of itself. While the priest was still asleep and quite unaware of all this, suddenly a head came cropping out of it, and legs and a tail appeared. And then this kettle jumped down from the box and began walking rather clumsily about the room.

One of the novices who had been in the next room all this time, thought that he heard a strange noise from his master's apartment, so he peeped in quietly. Fancy his astonishment at seeing the

tea-kettle walking about the room on its own feet! "Oh! horrors! Oh horrors!" he cried, "the tea-kettle is bewitched, it is bewitched!"

"What? the tea-kettle bewitched? Don't talk nonsense!" cried another novice peering in. But when he looked into the room his breath too was quite taken away. "Upon my word, this is astonishing! the tea-kettle has grown some feet and is beginning to walk!"

Then another exclaimed, "Look, it is turning towards us. It makes shivers run down my back!"

"It is nothing to be afraid of," said another, "I find it rather amusing. But his reverence seems to know nothing of this. Let us wake him and tell him about it."

So saying he went up to the priest and called out, " Your reverence, your reverence! An extraordinary thing has happened, something most marvellous."

"What is all this commotion about?" said the priest waking.

"No time to ask such questions," cried the young men, "only look and see. The tea-kettle has got some feet and is walking about the room."

"What! The tea-kettle has feet! Mercy on us!" he cried, rubbing his eyes and looking about.

But now behold, the tea-kettle was standing on its accustomed box looking quite as usual. So the priest would not believe what his disciples had told him and said, "What are you talking about, you foolish rascals? Isn't the kettle there, just where it ought to be?"

For the novices had not noticed till now that it had returned to its ordinary behaviour.

"Most astonishing," cried they, "our lives upon it, it was certainly walking about, a minute ago!"

"Well," replied the priest, "for all that, here it is on the box now and you don't suppose I am going to believe you. I have heard of wings sprouting from a pestle, but a tea-kettle with legs, that is something quite unheard of in any land. Confound you both for waking me up from my sound sleep with such prattle. Get out of my sight, you rascals."

The novices felt this reproof was rather unjust and they left the room muttering. But since they were quite satisfied that they had really seen the tea-kettle with legs, they could not rest until they could prove to their master that it was bewitched. Now on that very evening it happened that the priest was about to make tea alone. He filled the kettle with water and set it on the fire. Then as the water grew hotter, suddenly the kettle jumped off the hearth crying, "Too hot, too hot."

How astonished the priest was! "Alack, alack," he cried, "the kettle really is bewitched. Oh, come, some one, and catch it for me."

"There now!" exclaimed the disciples and they rushed to their master's assistance. They caught it at once, but by this time it was quite an ordinary kettle without legs or tail. However much they shook it or beat it, there was nothing but the clang of the metal, and no sign of magic.

"What an extraordinary purchase this was!" said the priest to himself, "I thought I had such a fine new kettle, but now when I use it, it causes such a commotion. What shall I do with it? There's no use keeping such a thing. I'll sell it at once; that will be the wisest plan."

On the very next day he sent for a rag-peddler and showed him the kettle. The peddler, of course, had not the slightest idea that there was anything at all unusual about it. "Why," he asked, "does your reverence wish to sell such a neat little kettle? Isn't it rather a pity?"

"Yes, you are right, it is a pity; but I have bought a better one, so I don't care for this any longer."

"Very well then, I will take it." So the peddler bought the kettle for four hundred *mon*,* and carried it home. The more he examined it, the more beautiful he found it. "What a treasure I have got!" he thought; and that night he went to bed in high spirits.

At about midnight, he heard a voice, whose he did not know, calling near his pillow, "Mr. Peddler! Mr. Peddler!" Wondering what it might be, he roused himself, and looked about. "What marvel is this?" he cried. "The kettle I bought to-day at Morinji is walking about the room, with a head and legs and tail!"

He was almost struck dumb with astonishment. "Well," he said addressing it, "Are you the kettle I bought to-day?"

---

* About forty *sen.*

At this the kettle came hopping, hopping towards the Peddler crying, "Are you frightened, Mr. Peddler?" "Frightened? Of course. Why shouldn't I be frightened? I thought you an ordinary little kettle. Who wouldn't be horrified to see a tea-kettle go walking about with a head and tail and hairy legs? What are you any way, a badger, or a bear, or a fox?"

The Tea-Kettle chuckled a little and answered, "Why, I am called the Tea-Kettle of Good-Luck, but I am really a badger in disguise."

"Then you aren't a real kettle at all?"

"No, I am not a real one, but I am

much nicer than a real one."

"How is that?"

"Since I bring good luck and am different from other kettles, you must bear this in mind when you use me and take great care of me. Then you will always be fortunate. But if, like the abbot of Morinji, you should fill me with water and set me

on the fire, as he did there—that would be too much."

"Of course. You are quite right," rejoined the Peddler, "but if I should leave you in your box, you would be very uncomfortable, and that would never do. What had I better do about it?"

"That is just the point," replied the Kettle. "If you took too great care of me and shut me up in this box, I should suffocate for lack of air. As I am alive, unless you often let me out and gave me something nice to eat, I should—"

"Yes, that would be hard lines," interrupted the Peddler.

"And so it was that at the temple, I was often very hungry and used to go creeping about in search of any poor pickings I might find, but at last those novices caught me and I only just escaped a beating. And now I suppose it was my fate that made me fall into your hands, and so I entrust myself to your kind care."

"Although I am poor I am a man and I cannot refuse your request. I will do my best for you," said the Peddler.

"Many thanks for your kindness," replied the Kettle, "but if I accept it, pray allow me in return to perform tricks for you."

"Perform tricks!" exclaimed the astonished old man. "You perform tricks! What kind?"

"I can dance," continued the Kettle, "and perform acrobatic feats."

"You can dance and perform acrobatic feats? That's splendid. Then I will give up peddling, and start a public-show with you as my performer, shall I not?"

"Yes, that's a capital idea. For if I work hard you will probably make far more money than by peddling."

"And I," added the Peddler, "will feed you well, so please do your best."

"That I will," returned the Kettle.

So the agreement was made, and they decided to open a show.

On the following day the Peddler began making preparations. First of all he built a show-house. Then he hired musicians and last of all he painted a sign-board to hang up in front of the house. When all this was done to his satisfaction, he put on his ceremonial dress and was quite ready to perform the duties of show-master.

At the entrance stood a crier. "Here," he shouted, "is to be seen an acrobatic Tea-Kettle performing entirely new and original tricks. It is quite different from a dog-show or the feats of a titmouse. In short, I will show you a kettle with a head, legs and a tail, dancing about. That, I assure you, is something unheard of in the history of the world. You will find it most entertaining. If you hesitate you may lose a chance in a thousand. You may pay your admission fee after

you have seen the performance, but when you have seen it, you will want to tell its wonders far and wide. Walk up! Walk up!"

Within, the Peddler opened the performance with these words: "I must beg you to excuse me for presuming to speak from this slightly elevated position. I am about to exhibit the performances of a magic tea-kettle. First we will show you a variety of dances, beginning with a rope-dance, and then a succession of other wonders. The performer will shortly make his appearance."

Immediately the Kettle came out upon the stage, and bowing slightly to the spectators began a rope-dance.

At sight of this astonishing spectacle, so much more wonderful than an ordinary creature on four legs, the spectators were dumbfounded and one after another were heard cries of, "Marvellous!" "Most amusing!" "Astonishing!"

The fame of the exhibition flew far and wide, and every one went to see it.

Every day the place was crowded with spectators, so that the building seemed in danger of tumbling down. Indeed the Kettle of Good-Luck had proved itself quite worthy of its name. In twenty days it had raised a fortune for its owner.

Now there was nothing miserly about this Peddler, and after a time he began to think that it must be rather dull for the performer to be at his tricks day in and day out. So one day he said "Bunbuku,* thanks to you, I am possessed of a fortune. I am more grateful than I can say, but I am quite satisfied with what I have. You must be tired of these incessant performances. I have made up

---

* Luck-bringer.

my mind to give up the exhibition. What do you think about it?"

"It will be quite agreeable to me if you wish it," replied the Tea-Kettle. "Then let me have my wish," said the Peddler.

And so immediately the exhibition was closed. Not long after this he took the Kettle and went to Morinji and told the priest all

its wonderful history. And besides that, he gave it back to him and with it half his fortune, saying, " It is really to you that I owe this good fortune, for you sold me the kettle and so I have come to thank you."

After this we hear of no more marvels but the Kettle was honoured with the name of the Tea-Kettle of Good-Luck and kept ever after at Morinji as its greatest treasure.

its wonderful history. And he liked that
he gave it back to him and with it both
his fortune, saying, "It is really to you
that I owe this good fortune, for you
sold me the kettle and so I have come to
thank you."

After this we hear of no more marvels,
but the Kettle was honoured with the
name of the Tea-Kettle
of good luck, and kept
ever after at Morin
its greatest
treasure.

KACHI-KACHI YAMA

IN olden days there lived an old man and woman. In their neighbourhood there was a mischievous old badger, who, coming out of his den every night, ravaged their fields and spoiled all the melons and egg-plants grown by the old man's hard labour and toil.

At last the old man, good-natured though he was, could not bear it any longer and said to himself—"I will make him repent of this one day." So he set a trap and caught the old badger.

"How glad I am! I have got rid of my trouble at last."

The old man, being much pleased, took

the badger to his home, and said to the old woman;

"I have caught the mischievous badger at last! See that it doesn't run away. In the evening we will have a meal of badger-soup."

The old man tying the four feet of the badger tightly together hung him up to the beam of the barn and went off to the field.

After he had gone, the badger, hanging from the beam of the barn, thinking and thinking how he could escape, made all sorts of wicked plans in his head.

Presently turning to the old woman, who was pounding wheat beside him, he said with pretended kindness;

"Surely it must be very tiring for an old woman like you to pound with such a heavy pestle. Hand it to me; I will pound it for you."

The old woman, shaking her gray-haired head, said,—"How can I do such a thing in the absence of my old man! How he would scold me if *anything* should happen! I am grateful for your kindness but I don't like to ask your help."

She was too clever to be deceived, but the badger, too, being an animal noted for its slyness, still went on trying to persuade her, saying in a coaxing voice;

"You are quite right to be so careful. But since I have been caught I will not run away or hide myself like a coward. If you think the old man will scold you for untying me, then you shall hang me up again as before, about the time you are expecting him home. Don't you think it will be safe if we do that? I will not run away. Just try for once and let me have the pestle."

Thus she was persuaded, good-natured old woman as she was, and thought to herself, "Since he asks so earnestly there can hardly be any danger."

So she released him and gave him

the pestle saying,—"Very well, you may pound for a while."

The badger, taking the pestle in his hand, made as if he would pound the wheat, but suddenly he struck the old woman with it! And when he was sure that she was dead he made soup out of her instead of the badger-soup. Then, disguising himself as the old woman and appearing quite unconcerned, he waited for the return of the old man.

The old man never dreamed that such a thing could happen during his absence and as he came along he said to himself,

"I could never have a happier day than this, for I have got rid of my trouble and moreover I can feast on badger-soup for a long time to come."

When he came back in very good spirits the badger, acting the part of the old woman, appeared to be waiting for

him impatiently, and said,—
"You are welcome! I have
been expecting you some
time and I have pre-
pared the badger-
soup."

He, being greatly pleased
to hear it, said, "Really! It is very good
of you to take so much trouble. I will
have it at once."

As soon as he had taken off his straw
sandals he sat down to the table, and not
knowing that the soup was made out of
the old woman, he had many bowls of it
showing how delicious he thought it was
by clicking his tongue.

By and by the badger, who had waited
upon the old man, suddenly showed
himself in his real form and said,—

"Old man, you have eaten the flesh
of your wife! Just look at the bones

underneath the sink!" And putting out
his tongue and tail together toward the
old man, ran away like a mist or cloud
leaving no trace behind him.

The old man was struck dumb with

horror and could not move at first but
at last recovering himself he said,—

"Poor old woman! So
the soup that I ate and
thought so delicious as
to click my tongue
over it was made
out of my old
woman!! How
I hate that
     badger! He shall see one day how
          I will take my revenge!"
               Overcome with remorse
               and grief, he threw him-
               self down and cried as
               if he were out of his
               senses.
               Presently he heard
               someone calling him
               above his head,
     "Dear old man! Why are you crying
so hard?"
     The old man wondered who was calling

him and lifting up his head, he saw an old white rabbit who was also living in the neighbourhood.

The white rabbit of course had a different nature from the old badger and as the old man knew that he was very good and kind he said, "Is it you, white rabbit? It is very kind of you to call on me! To tell the truth, my old woman was killed by the badger in such and such a way," telling him the story. "What greater sorrow could I have than this!"

The rabbit, hearing the whole story, felt very sorry for the old man and said,—

"This is very shocking but don't fret yourself so! As for avenging the old badger I will manage that for you. So only wait a little while patiently."

Thus the rabbit comforted him so that his heart was much eased and he said,—

"Among the same family of animals

some are very kind like you and some are wicked like the badger. But as providence never fails to help the good and punish the wicked, that rascal of a badger is sure to suffer from your revenge some day soon! I am looking forward to that day with joy."

"Yes, you may; since I promised you I will surely give you your revenge upon the rascal!"

Thus the rabbit, promising faithfully, went off to his home.

When the rabbit went back to his home he watched to see what his enemy was doing. Now the badger, after he had run away from the old man's house, afraid of being discovered, confined himself to the back part of his den.

Seeing this, the rabbit thought that he could not do anything unless he tricked the badger to come out of his den. Fortunately the next day was very fine. He called upon the badger in his den and said,—

"Mr. Badger, what is the matter with you that you shut yourself up on such a beautiful day! It is really rather lazy of you! Won't you come with me to the mountain to gather fire-wood?"

The badger never dreamed that he was going to be deceived, as the rabbit belonged to the same class of animals, so he replied;

"Yes, indeed! That will be very pleasant. I am a little tired of being here alone! Let us go off at once!"

They started off together for the mountain close by.

The rabbit having cleverly enticed the badger out of his hole, they wandered about the mountain together, gathering fire-wood when they pleased and carrying it on their shoulders. On the way back to their home the rabbit, perceiving that the badger was quite unaware of any danger, went behind him secretly and began to strike the flint that he had brought with him.

Then the badger pricking up his ears asked,—

"Mr. Rabbit, what was that the sound I heard just now behind me?"

"It's nothing! The name of this mountain is Kachi Kachi mountain; so I said 'Kachi Kachi.'"

While this conversation was going on the rabbit had struck fire from the flint and had kindled the bundle of fuel on the badger's back which now began to crackle.

The badger, hearing the sound, asked again,—

"Mr. Rabbit, what is the crackling

sound I hear behind me?"

"The sound? Oh, it's nothing! The name of this mountain is Bō Bō mountain; so I said 'Bō Bō.'"

Before the words were out of his mouth the fuel on the badger's back was all in a flame. The poor badger was terrified out of his wits!

"Oh! ho—o—o! This is dreadful! This is dreadful!" He cried rolling wildly about the ground in pain. The rabbit pretending to be very surprised, fanned him hard from behind. That made things still more un-

bearable for the badger and he, crying at the top of his voice, ran tumbling head over heels into his hole. The rabbit, looking on, felt only pleasure in the torments of the badger. The next day, putting on a very serious face, he went to inquire after his companion whom he found groaning in a state of great misery.

The rabbit taking out Tōgarashi-miso,* which he had brought with him, offered it to him saying,—

"Mr. Badger, I am very sorry that you met with such an accident yesterday! I have heard that this Tōgarashi-miso is the best remedy for a burn. I dare say it will hurt you a little, but won't you try it?"

The badger was very pleased and said; "It is very kind of you to bring it! Will you please be so kind as to put it on my back?" "All right."

And he put Tōgarashi-miso on the part where the flesh was raw so very thickly that it hurt the badger more than ever,

---

* A plaster of cayenne pepper.

and he rolled about his hole in terrible
agony.

Although he suffered so much, the
badger, stubborn fellow as he was, was
neither killed nor was his wicked mind
cured. So there is no need to pity him,
for death was what he deserved. While
the rabbit was thinking how he could
kill him, the badger, being much better,
came to call on him.

He saw the badger coming and said,—
"Oh, Mr. Badger, are you really better
now?"

"I am much better, thank you. The
pain has nearly gone."

"That's good. Then, shall we go for
a picnic again?"

"No, thank you. I have had enough
of picnics on the mountain."

"Then we will not go to the mountain
but to the sea this time."

"Yes, that might be very nice."

"I will make a boat for you; and when it is ready we will go for an expedition."

"Please arrange it as you think best," answered the badger, and he returned to his home.

After he had gone the rabbit set to work to make the boats, and in making them he had a design against the badger. He made his own boat of wood but the badger's of mud!

Two or three days after this, the badger came again to see him and asked,

"Have you made the boats?"

"Oh yes; I have them ready as you see."

"That's grand, shall we start at once?"

"Do you know how to row?"

"Of course!"

"Then let us start!"

They launched their boats and went far out to sea—the badger in his boat of mud, and the rabbit in his boat of wood.

"Mr. Badger, what a beautiful view we have near here!"

"Yes, indeed! The day is very fine and it is quite calm. It is very enjoyable, is it not?"

"But just to row about is not half so interesting as to have a race. Will you have one?" said the rabbit.

"Yes that will be fun!" answered the badger.

"Now we must put our boats in line. Let us start. One, two, three!"

The badger and the rabbit rowed with all their might, but the badger's boat being made of mud began absorbing water and crumbling away.

The badger noticed this now for the first time and cried out:

"Oh, what shall I do! what shall I

do! Please wait a little, Mr. Rabbit! My boat is dissolving! Save me! Save me!"

He was in such a panic crying loud for help.

The rabbit thought that this was the right moment to speak to the badger, so he stopped his boat and said,—

"Oh! You old rascal! You have killed our neighbour, the kind old woman and made soup out of her! Now receive your punishment from Heaven and prepare yourself to be killed!"

Thus saying he lifted his oar high and struck the badger on his head. The badger gave a shrill scream and sank down to the bottom of the sea.

Thus the rabbit killed the badger at last and fully avenged the old woman. He returned quickly to the old man's house and told him the whole story.

The old man was very pleased and told the rabbit that by his kind help his heart had been quite eased.

He praised the brave deed and as reward he gave him a grand feast. Afterwards he kept him in his house and loved him dearly as if he were his own son.

Medetashi! Medetashi!

JAPANESE FAIRY TALES
☆ 日本のお伽噺 ☆

昭和28年9月20日 初版発行　昭和55年6月30日 重版発行

編 者　北星堂編集部

発行所　株式会社 北星堂書店
　　　　代表者 中土順平

東京都千代田区神田錦町3丁目12番地
〒101 振替口座 東京 16024 番
電話 (03) 294-3301 (代表) 番

THE HOKUSEIDO PRESS
12, 3-Chome, Nishikicho, Kanda, Tokyo, Japan

Price ¥ **800** *in Japan*